JUNIOR NOVELIZATION

Simon Spotlight

New York   London   Toronto   Sydney   New Delhi

This book is a work of fiction. Any references to historical events, real people, or real places are used fictitiously. Other names, characters, places, and events are products of the author's imagination, and any resemblance to actual events or places or persons, living or dead, is entirely coincidental.

SIMON SPOTLIGHT
An imprint of Simon & Schuster Children's Publishing Division
1230 Avenue of the Americas, New York, New York 10020
DreamWorks Turbo © 2013 DreamWorks Animation L.L.C.
For information about special discounts for bulk purchases,
please contact Simon & Schuster Special Sales at 1-866-506-1949 or
business@simonandschuster.com.
Manufactured in the United States of America 0513 OFF
First Edition   2 3 4 5 6 7 8 9 10
ISBN 978-1-4424-8420-7
ISBN 978-1-4424-8421-4 (eBook)

Ready, Set . . . Turbo!

"And we're back at the final stretch of the Indianapolis 500 . . . and what a race it's been!" the announcer blared.

Engines roared and tires screeched as a sea of race cars zoomed around the track at the most important race in the world. A single red car blazed past the others.

"Guy Gagné is gaining on the pack," the announcer reported. "The young French Canadian is making quite an impression in his debut here at the Motor Speedway. In all my years of racing, I've never seen a driver with this much raw talent!"

Thousands of fans in the stands cheered on

Guy as he raced for the finish line. And in a dusty Southern California garage, Guy's biggest fan watched the race on videotape. He'd seen it over and over again.

Guy's biggest fan also happened to be his smallest fan. His name was Turbo, and he was a tiny orange garden snail. His brown shell was adorned with decals from an old toy car: a black-and-white-checked racing flag, and a faded number five. Two round, curious eyes peered out from the tops of his flexible eyestalks.

Turbo loved to imagine that he was in the race too. His shell would be polished and adorned with real sponsor logos, just like the big racers. He would speed down the track, kicking up clouds of dust behind him.

"He's gaining on the pack!" Turbo imagined the announcer would say. "Moving into fourth position . . . third . . . now second! It's neck and neck! And it looks like the winner is . . . Turbo!"

Turbo could practically hear the roar of the crowd cheering for him. "Turbo! Amazing! Unbelievable!

Instant replay! Turbo! Turbo! Turbo!"

Turbo hit the fast-forward button on the remote. The video skipped forward to the post-race interview. Turbo loved this part. He pictured himself in front of the cameras, bragging about his victory.

"What inspired you to become a race driver?" the reporter asked.

"Well, I'm glad you asked me that," Turbo replied smoothly. "Everyone's got that one thing that makes them happy. For me . . . it's *terrifying, terrifying, blazing speed.*"

"Theo!" an annoyed voice interrupted him.

Turbo turned to see his older brother, Chet, on the windowsill of the garage. A chubby purple snail, Chet refused to call Turbo by his chosen name. Theo was the name he was born with, but Turbo was the name of the snail he wanted to be.

Turbo pretended that Chet was another reporter at the race.

"Yes, the handsome fellow in the back," Turbo replied.

"What are you doing?" Chet asked with a yawn.

"What I've always done—stay focused and try to run my race," Turbo answered. "That's all any driver can do. Next question."

Chet did not want to play along. "Can you please go to sleep?" he asked. "We've got work tomorrow."

"Sleep? Are you kidding me?" Turbo asked. "It takes *hours* to come down after a big race like this."

"Yeah, I bet," Chet replied, pulling his head back inside his shell.

Turbo turned back to the TV. The reporter was still talking to Guy.

"Guy, when you were just a rookie, starting out in the Indy Lights, did you ever dream you'd be standing here today?" he asked.

Guy smiled. "Well, as my dear father always told me, no dream is too big, and no dreamer . . ."

"Too small!" Turbo finished with him.

Turbo's heart soared every time he heard that. It was just how he felt inside. So what if he was small? So what if he was a snail? He could still dream of being fast—fast enough to win the Indy 500, just like his hero.

"Sleep!" Chet yelled.

But Turbo ignored him. He knew that in order to achieve his dream, he'd have to train hard, just like the pros. He moved over to the practice track he had made for himself. The track was a yardstick—exactly three feet long. To time himself, he used an old clock.

The clock hit 2:00 a.m., and Turbo took off. He zoomed down the track as fast as he could, imagining himself on the Indy racetrack. When he reached the end of the yardstick, he collapsed, exhausted. Then he looked at the clock, which read 2:17.

"Yessss! Seventeen minutes! That's a new record!" he cheered.

"Theo!" Chet yelled.

Turbo sighed and curled up inside his shell. There was always tomorrow. . . .

A Day at the Plant

The next morning Turbo and Chet made their way to work, along with the other snails who lived in the same backyard. They slowly trudged down the garden path in a long line.

"Let's go, people! Pick it up!" Turbo yelled.

He scanned the line of snails in front of him, looking for an opening. He spotted a space between two snails.

"Turbo, ready to make his move. . . ," he said, pretending to be a race announcer.

He surged forward, but another snail crossed his path at the last second. She bumped into him, and he slid back to Chet.

"Did you see that? She cut me off!" Turbo asked.

Chet chuckled. He thought his little brother's racing obsession was funny. "Ah, the joys of racing," he said sarcastically. "How could anyone not see the appeal of watching a bunch of cars drive around in circles for hours on end? Left turn . . . left turn . . . left turn!"

Turbo sighed. "Your ignorance saddens me to no end, Chet."

Chet enjoyed teasing him. "Left turn! Oh, what do I do here? Oh no, wait a minute . . . left turn!"

The brothers arrived at the plant entrance. It was a tomato plant, to be exact, and the snails worked hard all day to harvest the delicious tomatoes.

A teapot whistled inside the house behind them, signaling the start of the day. Turbo hated working at the plant, but Chet loved it. He loved the order of it, and most of all he loved being in charge of safety.

Feeling chipper, he scooted ahead of Turbo and climbed up the thick green tomato stalk. He slowly made his way to the sunny leaves on top and talked to the workers there.

"All right, people, we've got a lot of tomatoes to

harvest today," Chet said. "We gotta pick 'em, we gotta sort 'em, we gotta eat 'em, but most importantly, we gotta be . . ."

"Safe!" the workers finished for him.

"Yes!" Chet said. "Music to my ears!"

He slid over to a group of workers who were staring up at a tomato.

"Look at her!" one exclaimed.

Chet looked up. "Hello, Big Red," he said. "You are one juicy temptress."

The tomato was the biggest, ripest, plumpest tomato on the plant. The stem looked ready to snap. Now all they had to do was wait . . . and snails were very good at waiting.

Except for Turbo, that is. He waited on the ground, bored, next to a ramp made of ice-pop sticks. When a tomato fell, it would roll down the ramp, and Turbo and other workers would push it over to the cleaning station.

"Any day now," Turbo mumbled.

Then one of the workers overhead yelled, "Overripe!"

Turbo looked up to see a brown, bruised tomato

slowly rolling down the ramp.

Turbo tried to scoot away. "Oh no!"

Splat! The rotten tomato rolled onto Turbo and collapsed in a juicy heap.

With a sigh, Turbo shrugged off the stinky mess. Then he picked up two twigs and made a barrier in front of him.

"Here we go," he said, looking up.

"Overripe!"

Two more rotten tomatoes rolled down the ramp. *Splat!* They knocked down the barrier and exploded all over Turbo.

The next time a rotten tomato came down the ramp, Turbo hopped out of the way.

"Not this time!" he said.

But the tomato hit a bump. It rolled right back toward Turbo.

Splat! Sticky tomato goo covered him again!

He gave the next tomato plenty of room. This time, it didn't hit a bump. Turbo got behind it and started to push it toward the cleaning station.

How boring, Turbo thought. *This is even worse than*

getting hit by a rotten tomato! I'd rather be racing.

That gave him an idea. He used his tail to draw a "01" on the side of the tomato.

"And the cars are at the starting line," he said in his announcer voice. "Guy Gagné's in the top pole position, driving his trademark number 01 overripe tomato. Next to him is that feisty young upstart, Turbo."

Then he changed his voice. "Gentlemen, start your engines!"

Turbo gave the tomato a push toward the cleaning station. Then he slid next to it, pretending to race it.

"Guy rolls into the lead around the first turn with Turbo hot on his tail," Turbo announced.

Some of the workers rolled their eyes.

"There he goes again," said one snail, with a snicker.

Turbo didn't care. He was having fun. "They're neck and neck. Guy . . . Turbo . . . Guy . . . Turbo . . ."

The snail workers started a mocking chant. "Turbo . . . Turbo . . . Turbo!"

Turbo let the other snails get to him. Embarrassed,

he stopped racing and scooted back to his station.

"Overripe!"

Splat! Another rotten tomato exploded on Turbo.

A foreman came up to Chet, looking fed up.

"Talk to your brother, Chet," he said. "Or I will."

"I'm on it, Carl. This will not happen again," Chet promised.

"Uh-huh. Heard that before," the foreman said, sliding away. Chet looked at Turbo and shook his head.

After a long morning of pushing tomatoes, it was time for lunch. Most of the workers sat on the sunny leaves, enjoying their tomato slices. Turbo glumly ate his lunch alone on a dead branch in the shade.

"You do this to yourself, you know," Chet said. He nodded at the racing decals on his brother's shell. "I mean, look at you. How could they not make fun of you? It's almost like you're forcing them."

Turbo didn't say anything.

"If you'd just quit it with the speed stuff," Chet said.

"I can't help it," Turbo told him. "It's in me."

"Hmm, no. It's *not* in you," Chet informed him.

Turbo frowned. "Says who?"

"Nature. Mother Nature. Maybe you've heard of her?" Chet looked into his brother's eyes. "We all have our limitations, Theo. And the sooner you accept the dull, miserable reality of your existence, the happier you'll be."

"Wow. Aren't you a ray of sunshine," Turbo said sarcastically.

Then they heard the sound of a garage door opening. A boy sitting on a tricycle rolled out. He looked like every snail's worst nightmare, with his sunglasses, his helmet, and his giant wheel of doom.

A lookout snail let out a cry. "Heads up! Shell crusher, two o'clock!"

The boy started to roll down the driveway.

Squish! He rolled right over an unlucky cockroach.

"All right people, you know the drill!" Chet yelled. "Tuck and roll!"

Every snail stopped what they were doing and tucked into their shell—every snail but Turbo.

"Theo, tuck and roll!" Chet growled, annoyed.

Turbo glared at Tricycle Boy. "We've been over this. I don't tuck and roll."

"You have a shell for a reason. Use it!" Chet snapped.

"*You* use it," Turbo shot back. "He's not even looking this way!"

He scooted out to the edge of his leaf. "Hey, Juice Box! Nice tricycle!" he yelled at the kid.

Frustrated, Chet yanked on Turbo's tail, pulling him away from the edge. He watched as Tricycle Boy rolled away from the garden to the front of the house.

"All right, good hustle, good hustle, everybody!" he yelled to the workers. Then he glared at Turbo. "*Almost* everybody."

The teakettle inside the house whistled again, and Turbo was happy for the first time all day.

"Quitting time!" he cheered.

Then he hurried back to the garage as fast as he could . . . for a snail.

Nooooooooo!

"Honey! I'm home!" Turbo yelled cheerfully as he inched into the garage.

He was talking to the old TV, of course. He hopped on the remote and the TV clicked on.

Turbo took a sip of Adrenalode (Guy Gagné's favorite energy drink) from a straw. His stomach grumbled as the drink hit his belly.

"Ugh!" he said. "That tasted . . . awesome."

The next part of the video showed Guy being interviewed by a sportscaster.

"I love you, Guy!" Turbo yelled at the screen.

"Tell us, Guy, do you have any advice for future racers who might be watching at home right now?" the sportscaster asked.

Turbo scooted closer to the screen, dragging the can of Adrenalode with him.

"Oh my gosh, that's me! That's me!" he said.

Guy looked into the camera. "Well, there comes a time in every race when a driver is forced to make that one split-second decision: fall behind, or push ahead."

"Push ahead!" Turbo cheered.

"To take a chance and risk it all . . . or play it safe and suffer defeat," Guy continued.

Turbo bounced up and down with excitement, and the can began to wobble.

"Risk it all, Guy!" Turbo yelled.

"But what really separates the racers from the champions . . ."

Turbo was surprised. He always clicked off the tape at this point. He never realized there was more to the interview.

"That one thing that separates the ordinary from the extraordinary . . . ," Guy teased.

"What is it?" Turbo asked impatiently. He bounced up and down, and the Adrenalode can fell off the table. The drink splashed onto the frayed TV cord.

"That one thing is . . ."

Fffzzzttt! The frayed cord sparked, and the TV went black!

"Noooooo!" Turbo wailed.

He inched closer to the television. "No, you didn't! No! Please come back!"

He pushed the power button over and over again with his foot.

"No! No! No!"

He pounded the screen with his eyeballs, hoping to jolt the TV back to life. Each time he hit it, the TV moved closer to the edge of the table. But Turbo didn't realize that.

"Come! Back! To! Me! T! V!" Turbo pleaded.

The TV began to slide off the table. Only the cord plugged into the wall kept it from falling. Desperate, Turbo grabbed the cord in his mouth. He reached around with his foot to steady it. Suddenly, the TV flickered back on.

"The one thing is . . . ," Guy was saying, and then . . .

"It's working!" Turbo cried. He forgot the cord was in his mouth.

Crash! The plug popped out of the outlet, and the television set crashed to the floor.

"Noooooo!" Turbo howled.

Now he would never hear Guy's advice. He would never know the secret to becoming an Indy 500 racer.

I guess my racing dreams are over, Turbo thought sadly.

Turbo vs. the Lawn Mower

The next morning Turbo waited at the end of the tomato ramp, lost in another daydream.

"Overripe!" a worker yelled overhead.

Turbo didn't hear him.

Splat! A rotten tomato rolled down the ramp and exploded all over him. Turbo didn't even feel it. He was imagining a race between himself and Guy Gagné. They were neck and neck. . . .

"Lunch!"

With a sigh Turbo followed Chet to the lunch line. They each got a slice of tomato and then settled on a low branch. Turbo didn't feel like eating, but Chet munched away happily.

"You know, this is good," Chet said thoughtfully.

Turbo gave Chet a funny look. How could his broken TV be a good thing?

"With that TV gone, you can finally get out of that garage," Chet went on. "You can put all that racing behind you!"

"And do what?" Turbo asked.

"Start living your life," Chet replied.

Turbo sighed. "I have a life?"

Suddenly the branch they were on began to tilt. They saw a flash of red through the leaves.

"Big Red?" Chet wondered. The big juicy beauty was hanging down low, ready to drop.

A cry went out among the snails.

"Big Red! Big Red!"

Big Red snapped off its branch and began to roll down the vine. It hit the dirt and then bounced, landing on the lawn just outside the plant. The plant workers let out a cheer.

The workers lined up on the little brick wall at the garden's edge, eagerly eyeing the tomato.

"Let's go chow down!" one worker yelled.

"Whoa, hit the brakes, people," Chet said. "It's Gardener Day."

He nodded toward the driveway, where the gardener had parked his truck and was unloading his lawn mower.

The plant workers nodded, sighed in disappointment, and slowly shuffled off. Getting Big Red was just too dangerous.

Turbo climbed onto the wall. "You're quitting? Just like that?" he asked in disbelief. How could they give up on the biggest, best tomato from the plant?

One of the workers shrugged. "Nothing ventured, nothing gained."

"That's a *bad* thing!" Turbo said.

Turbo turned toward the lawn. The gardener hadn't even started mowing yet. And Big Red sat just a few feet away. He knew what he had to do.

"There comes a time in every race when a driver is forced to make that one split-second decision," Turbo began, remembering what Guy Gagné had said. "Take a chance and risk it all . . . or play it safe and suffer defeat."

"I'm seeing defeat here," one of the workers called out with a laugh.

Chet inched up to Turbo. "Okay, enough with the crazy talk. Just get back to work."

Defiant, Turbo hopped off the little wall and onto the grass.

Chet yelled after him as Turbo eyed his big red prize and started talking in his announcer voice.

"And the cars are at the starting line. Gentlemen, start your engines!"

The lawn mower roared to life and Turbo scooted out onto the lawn. In his mind, he zoomed through the grass at a hundred miles per hour, leaving the lawn mower in the dust.

In real life the lawn mower was moving steadily toward Turbo. It was only a matter of time before the two would collide.

But Turbo imagined he was on a racetrack with a crowd cheering him on. Turbo blazed past the other cars, heading for the finish line.

Chet watched in horror as the lawn mower bore down on his brother.

"Tuck and roll! Tuck and roll!"

Turbo snapped out of his fantasy just as the mower's sharp, shiny blades appeared above him. His eyes widened as he realized the horrible truth. He wasn't going to make it to Big Red in time.

Whoosh! A powerful blast of water knocked Turbo across the lawn. Chet and the other workers had turned on the garden hose just in time.

Turbo looked back at Big Red. Now that he was safe, he could still try to get the prize.

Sploosh! The lawn mower rolled over it, and Big Red exploded, spraying tomato juice everywhere.

Chet charged toward Turbo. "Are you insane? You could've gotten yourself killed! What were you thinking?"

Turbo looked from his brother to the other plant workers, who stared at him angrily.

"I thought I could get there," Turbo said meekly.

Chet shook his head in dismay. "When are you gonna wake up?"

Turbo couldn't answer. He lowered his head and slowly shuffled away.

Turbo Transforms

Turbo kept inching away from the garden, away from the garage, and out into the street. He just kept going and going.

Night fell as Turbo made his way across an overpass. He inched his way along the guardrail and then looked down at a highway below.

Speeding cars whizzed by in an ocean of light and sound. Turbo stared, transfixed at the sight of all the fast vehicles. Cars, trucks, motorcycles . . . each one seemed faster than the last.

It was a magic moment. Turbo looked up at the stars in the night sky and then closed his eyes.

"I wish . . . I wish I was built for speed," Turbo whispered.

He opened his eyes, hoping to find that he had transformed into a sleek racing car. But he was just the same old Turbo.

Defeated, he turned around. He might as well head back home. But then . . .

Honk! An eighteen-wheeler rumbled across the overpass at breakneck speed. A blast of rushing wind sent Turbo tumbling off the guardrail. He sailed down to the dry concrete waterway below, on the side of the highway.

Turbo landed on the cement slope and bounced a few times, landing safely.

"Whew, that was close," Turbo said, relieved.

Then he heard a cheering crowd and saw a black-and-white checkered flag waving in front of him. Turbo looked down to see that he had landed on top of a race car!

Turbo didn't know it, but he had landed right in the middle of a drag race. He had landed on top of a powerful race car. A souped-up racing import revved its engines right next to him.

Before Turbo could react, the flag dropped.

"Oh no!" Turbo screamed.

He hung on for dear life as the race car sped down the waterway.

Then pure joy replaced the fear. This was fast! *Really* fast! Faster than he'd ever felt before!

His soul soared with the feeling, and he howled with delight. He had never felt more alive. Looking to his right, he saw the import pull ahead of them.

"No!" Turbo yelled. "Come on, faster!"

The driver slammed his foot on the gas.

Whoosh! The engine's air-intake valve sucked Turbo inside!

Shrieking, Turbo flew through the engine's pipes like a runaway pinball.

Turbo splashed into the engine's fuel, struggling to stay afloat. The driver of the race car had no idea that he had a helpless snail inside his engine. He just wanted to win. He put his finger on a red button on his dashboard. One push of the button would send nitrous oxide into the engine, giving him the extra burst of speed he would need to win the race.

Turbo thrashed around frantically, trying to get

out, when the driver pressed the button.

Whoosh! The nitrous oxide exploded out of the canister, through the engine block, and into the combustion chamber. The nitrous blast zapped Turbo, charging his body with blue energy. It surged into his bloodstream, and fused with his cells.

Blam! Turbo shot out of the car's tailpipe, sailed over the ground, and crashed into the cement wall.

Hours later Turbo opened his eyes. He could see three black crows circling high above him.

"Ah!" With a cry, he slid into an empty Chinese food carton. Using it to shield himself, he began to inch his way home.

As he moved, he thought about the night before. Did it really happen? It seemed like a crazy dream.

Turbo crawled and crawled until he found himself back on the sidewalk. He shrugged off the carton and saw the garage in front of him.

"Home," he said with a sigh.

When he entered the garage, he scooted up to a hubcap to check out his reflection. To his great relief, everything looked fine.

"I'm okay. Whew!" he said, closing his eyes.

When he opened them again, two headlight beams shone back at him from the hubcap. "Oh . . . that's peculiar," Turbo said.

Confused, Turbo looked back at the hubcap.

The lights were coming from his eyes. But that was impossible!

He turned one eye toward the other, blinding himself.

"Aaahhh!" Both lights went out.

Freaked out, Turbo backed away from the hubcap. Suddenly his shell started to flash and beep like a car alarm. He quickly realized it was coming from him!

"Oh no, stop, stop, stop!" he cried, craning his neck to look at his shell. "Quiet! Quiet! Stop it!"

He frantically smacked his shell into the leg of the worktable, and the alarm stopped. Turbo sighed with relief, but then worry flooded him again.

"What's happening to me?" he wondered.

Tricycle Battle

Still worried, Turbo inched his way to the plant. The workers had gathered for an afternoon safety meeting led by Chet.

"I would like to begin with some very exciting news," Chet said. "The latest figures are in: Accidental smashes were down fifteen percent this month. Well done, team."

The workers applauded, clapping their eyeballs together. Turbo joined in, but then his eyestalks began to pick up a radio station. The sound came right out of his mouth!

"Yo, yo, yo, we're listening to 98.6 where hip-hop bricky-bricky beats!" said the deejay.

Terrified, Turbo quickly shut his mouth and the music stopped. Everyone looked at Turbo, confused, and he slowly backed away.

As he made his way back to the garage, Turbo experimented with his radio powers. He moved his eyestalks and got a new radio station, and the new music blasted from his mouth again.

At the same time, the little boy on the tricycle rode out of the garage. Hearing the music, he spotted Turbo sliding out of the grass onto the driveway. Turbo smacked his eyes together quickly, and the sound instantly went off.

"Ah, finally!" Turbo remarked.

Then he became aware of a growing shadow looming over him. Looking up, he saw the front tire of the tricycle bearing down on him like a steamroller!

Adrenaline raced through his body. His shell lit up with a blast of blue light.

Whoosh! The tricycle ran right over him. Or did it? The boy looked down, hoping to see a squished snail, but he was disappointed.

Stunned, Turbo looked behind him to see a

sizzling trail of blue light streaming across the driveway. Did he do that?

He didn't have time to think about it, because the tricycle boy had turned around, ready to crush Turbo again. Blue light ignited under Turbo's shell, and he zipped in front of the wheel, missing it again.

The tricycle boy frowned, angry that he had missed the snail again. Turbo couldn't believe it either. The boy kept coming, and Turbo zipped around the driveway, avoiding each attack.

Out of control, Turbo smashed through the plank of a wooden fence. He flew up, landed on the plank, and then slid down it like a ramp. The ramp sent him right on top of the tricycle's front tire.

A sinister smile came across the boy's face as he prepared to squish Turbo once and for all. Turbo floored it, and his superspeed caused the front wheel to spin with amazing force. The back of the tricycle actually lifted off the ground!

The boy screamed in fear as Turbo spun the front wheel faster and faster. The tricycle bucked, and the boy went flying off! Terrified, he jumped to his feet and ran into the house, screaming for his mother.

"Oh yeah!" Turbo cheered.

But without the boy weighing down the tricycle, Turbo couldn't control it. The tricycle bounced down the grassy slope leading to the garden—right in the direction of the plant!

Chet was still speaking when he saw it.

"Tuck and roll!" Chet screamed.

But it was too late.

Slam! Snails and tomatoes went flying as the tricycle crashed into the plant. It finally landed upside down, wheels spinning. Turbo rolled off the tricycle unhurt. But the damage had been done.

Turbo arrived back at the plant just as the dust cleared. The plant was a wreck. Clean-up crews pushed broken branches and squashed tomatoes out of the way. Carl spotted Turbo and glared at him angrily.

Turbo grinned sheepishly at the foreman. "I admit that there's a wee bit of damage to your inventory, but if you just let me explain—"

"You're fired!" Carl barked.

Chet scooted up. "Whoa, Carl. Just calm down.

If you just give him one more chance, I promise that this will never, ever—"

"You don't understand," Carl said, circling the brothers. "*You're* fired. You, plural. Both of you!"

Chet stared, shocked, as Carl slid away.

"Chet, I'm so sorry," Turbo said.

Chet turned to him. "All my life I've defended you," he said. "I've covered for you, stood up for you, apologized for you. And this is what I get in return."

Turbo felt terrible. "I'm really sorry."

"What is *wrong* with you?" Chet yelled.

"I don't know," Turbo replied thoughtfully. "All I know is—"

"*I didn't really want an answer!*" Chet yelled. "*I already know!*"

High overhead a crow heard Chet's scream. It swooped down, grabbed Chet in its beak, and flew away.

"Help! The world is moving!" Chet shrieked.

In a flash, blue light ignited inside Turbo's shell. He had to save his brother!

The Snail Races

Chet screamed in horror as the crow flew through the trees. Down below, Turbo tore down the sidewalk, keeping his eyes on the sky.

Chet didn't see his brother. All he could see was the house and the plant disappearing in the distance as the crow flew away. Then two crows swooped in on either side. Chet knew what they wanted: him!

Chet closed his eyes. "Okay, I'm going to wake up any minute now. Wake up! Wake up!"

One of the crows dive-bombed the crow holding Chet, knocking him loose.

"Aaaaaahhh!" he screamed as he plummeted toward the ground. "Somebody help me!"

The third crow grabbed Chet in his beak, flying down toward a busy intersection.

Turbo raced into the street, charging past the cars as he tried to catch up to the crows. Overhead, the crow carrying Chet landed on top of a run-down taco truck. It dropped Chet onto the metal roof, ready to scarf down its prey.

But the other two crows landed on the truck and stared at the third, daring it to make a move.

"Easy now, fellas," Chet said as the crows inched closer to him. "You really don't want to do this."

The three crows pounced all at once. Chet's instincts kicked in, and he tucked inside his shell.

He didn't see the flash of blue light tear across the truck roof. Turbo had arrived!

One of the crows quickly scooped Turbo inside its mouth. Turbo revved up, pulling the crow all over the truck and slamming him against the windshield. Then he blasted out of its mouth, and the crow flew off, followed by the others.

Chet, meanwhile, had no idea what had just happened.

"Am I dead? Is this heaven?" he asked, slowly coming out of his shell. He looked around at the dirty sidewalk. "I pictured it . . . cleaner."

Turbo scooted up to him. "Come on, get up."

Chet couldn't believe his eyes. "Oh no, did the crows get you, too?"

"What?" Turbo asked. "No, it wasn't the crows."

Beeeeep! A car horn blared as it roared past. Chet got a better look at his surroundings.

"Look at this place. Broken glass, rusty nails," he said, his voice rising in panic. For a snail, those things could be deadly.

"Just breathe," Turbo told him.

Chet turned his head. "Discarded salt packets . . ." Every snail knows that salt could shrivel a snail into oblivion. "It's like a minefield out here!"

"Chet, there is no reason to panic," Turbo assured him. "Everything is going to be just fine."

Clunk! A clear jar came down on top of them, trapping them! Turbo and Chet looked up to see the chubby face of a Mexican American guy grinning down at them.

"Well, well, well. *Buenas noches*, little amigos," he said. "This must be my lucky day."

He carried the jar into his truck and placed it down. Then he dialed a number on his cell phone.

"*Hola.* It's Tito," he said. "Tell everyone I'm bringing it!"

Turbo and Chet looked at each other, too frightened to speak. Who was this guy, and where was he taking them?

The truck pulled into a strip mall. The worn sign was shaped like a shooting star with the words STARLIGHT PLAZA underneath. Half of the stores were closed, but a few were open: a nail salon, a hobby shop, an auto body shop, and a restaurant called Dos Bros Tacos.

Tito parked the truck near the garage of the auto body shop. The brothers could see a group of people gathered in the shadows in the back of the garage. Tito picked up the jar and hopped out of the truck.

"Somebody better call the cops, 'cause I'm about to make a killing!" he announced.

Three people walked up to Tito. Kim-Ly, the owner

of the nail salon, carefully eyed the two new snails inside the jar.

"Ha! Whiplash is going to eat them up!" the woman said.

Chet gave a frightened yelp. It sounded like these people were going to make a meal of him and Turbo.

Bobby, the owner of the hobby shop, nodded his head. "It's gonna be a slaughter," he agreed.

Paz, a young mechanic who owned the body shop, grinned slyly. "Yeah, dead meat!"

Chet retreated inside his shell. "We're gonna die. We're gonna die," he repeated worriedly.

Turbo scanned the garage, trying to figure out what was going on. He spotted a chalkboard with names scrawled on it: "Skidmark," "Burn," "White Shadow," "Whiplash," and "Smoove Move." There were numbers underneath the names that looked like odds on a betting form, like he had seen in a newspaper once.

Paz hit a button and a makeshift racetrack rose from the floor. It was a straight shot from start to finish. Bobby doused it with water to make it slick.

As Tito spilled Turbo and Chet out of the jar and

onto the starting line, Bobby placed a snail next to Turbo. Turbo had never seen a snail like him. He had a sleek, dark purple body, and it looked like he had a tiny racing motor attached to his shell!

The snail looked at Turbo and sneered. "Little far from home, aren't you, garden snail?"

Then Kim-Ly placed a blue snail next to Chet. This one was small and lean, with a shell tricked out to look like a drag racer. Chet shivered in fear.

"Hey, I think we got a crier here," the blue snail cracked.

Turbo's mind whirred as he tried to figure out what was happening. Three more snails were added to the starting line. One was pink with a pair of dice around his neck. The other was big and white, and the fattest snail Turbo had ever seen. The third was fiery red with yellow flames painted on her shell and a chrome exhaust pipe.

The snails started to psyche themselves up.

"Let's do this!"

"I got this one!"

Chet tried to make a break for it. He scooted

away, but Tito's hand reached down and placed him firmly back by the starting line. Then Tito held up a red bandanna.

"Ready . . ."

The snails started to make engine noises, like they were getting ready for a race.

"Set . . ."

That's when it dawned on Turbo. He and Chet were about to be in a snail race!

"Go!"

Tito dropped the flag, and the snails started to scoot down the track. Chet tried to scoot in the opposite direction, but Tito turned him around again.

Turbo rolled his eyes. These snails might have tricked-out shells, but they were just as slow as the snails back home. What was the point of racing them?

Then Kim-Ly pointed at Turbo. "Ha-ha! Look. He dead! Taco Man found dead snail!" The other shopkeepers began to laugh along with her.

Tito's face turned red, but Turbo started to turn a different color—blue. The blue energy inside him began to rev up. Dead snail? He would show them!

Tito looked at him then and saw the determination in Turbo's eyes. He stared at the little snail, stunned. And then . . .

Boom! Turbo took off like a rocket, blasting down the track and knocking down the other racers like they were bowling pins. The laughter stopped, and Tito's eyes widened as he watched Turbo tear across the finish line.

Turbo couldn't stop himself. He blazed out of the garage and across the parking lot like a neon bullet. Then he circled back to the track.

"Santa Maria," Tito said in disbelief.

The racing snails inched toward Turbo, impressed.

"What did you say your name was again?" asked the blue snail.

Turbo paused. Chet and the other snails knew him as Theo. But in his heart, he had always known his true name.

"My name . . . is Turbo," he said proudly.

Turbo Gets Schooled

The racing snails crowded around Turbo.

"Where did you come from?" asked the blue one.

"How'd you do that?" asked the red one.

Chet stared at his brother, worried.

"I'd like a word with you please," he said, pulling Turbo aside. "Okay, that was . . ."

"Amazing, right?" Turbo said, still pumped up from the race.

Chet gave his brother a concerned hug. "It's okay. Just hang in there. As soon as we get home, we're gonna get you fixed."

Turbo pulled back. "What? I don't need to be fixed. There's nothing wrong with me, Chet!"

"Nothing wrong with you?" Chet repeated. "You're . . . you're a freak of nature!"

"I know! I know!" Turbo said, grinning. "Isn't it great?"

Before Chet could respond, Tito scooped up Turbo and hoisted him into the air on his palm. He looked at Turbo fondly.

"I don't know what crazy lab you escaped from, but you are amazing, little amigo. Amazing!" he said, his brown eyes shining.

"Tito!"

Tito turned to see his older brother, Angelo, standing in the garage doorway. Both brothers sported goatees and had slicked-back black hair, but Angelo was a little shorter and a little leaner than Tito. He wore a white half-apron over his yellow Dos Bros Tacos T-shirt.

Angelo pointed out the door to the sign for Dos Bros Tacos. "Do you see that sign, Tito? What does it say?"

"Angelo—" Tito started to protest.

"It says, 'Dos Bros Tacos.' *Dos* Bros, Tito, as in you and me. Not *Uno* Bros," Angelo reminded him. "You're supposed to be out there selling tacos, not racing snails."

"I know, but this little guy is something special," Tito said, holding up Turbo. "I'm telling you, Angelo, the customers are gonna be lining up around the block! I can see it already . . . 'Come for the Snail Racing, Stay for the Chimichangas!'"

"Get your head out of the clouds, Tito," Angelo told him. "It's enough with your crazy schemes."

Tito shook his head. "No. You are a taco genius, Angelo. And it's my mission in life to share your gift with the world!"

"Great," Angelo said dryly. "Then first thing in the morning, get in that truck and go sell some tacos!"

He turned and stormed back to the taco shop. Tito, deflated, looked down at Turbo, who gave him a sympathetic nod.

Tito said good-bye to the other shop owners and carried Turbo into the taco shop. Ignored, Chet slowly followed them. When he finally scooted onto the shop counter, he couldn't believe what he saw. Tito had set out a Mexican feast for Turbo: tacos, nachos, guacamole, and salsa. Chet got hungry just looking at it.

"Are you tired?" Tito asked Turbo. "Here, I made your bed."

Tito had piled a stack of napkins as a bed for Turbo, and added a fluffed-up ketchup packet as a pillow. Grateful, Turbo climbed onto the mattress.

"Now, it might get a little chilly tonight, so I warmed up your blanket," Tito said. He pulled a tortilla out of a tortilla warmer and gently placed it over Turbo, tucking him in.

"There you go, all comfy and cozy," he said. Then he leaned down and gave Turbo a kiss on the shell. "Sweet dreams, little amigo. I'll see you in the morning."

Chet scooted up to the bed. "Did he really just kiss you good night?"

"He did. Jealous?" Turbo asked.

Thump! Thump! Thump! Thump! Thump! Five shadowy figures landed on the windowsill outside. The window panel swiveled, revealing the racing snails.

"Question. What gives with the superspeed?" asked the blue snail.

"Hey. Hey. You a robot?" asked the red snail, quickly circling him.

"Is it contagious?" asked the big white one.

The dark purple snail inched up. "Give the kid some space," he said. Then he looked right at Turbo. "I'm Whiplash. And this here is my crew."

The blue snail slid down a soda bottle, making a loud, skidding noise as he moved. He had a yellow number thirteen on his blue shell. Like the other snails, his shell had been tricked out with toy car parts: chrome exhaust pipes and a tall spoiler attached to the back of his shell, just like race cars used to keep them steady on the track.

"I'm Skidmark!" he announced.

The red snail scooted next to Turbo. "And I'm Burn!" Fake flames shot out of her exhaust pipes. "Sizzle, sizzle, uh-huh!"

The pink snail with the fuzzy dice around his neck glided next to Burn. He had a green shell decked out like a lowrider.

"The name's Smoove Move," he said. "I set the tone around here, you dig? Now check this, right about now I'm movin' so fast the whole world's goin' in slow motion, baby."

Smoove Move slid across the floor slowly, but he made a face like he was moving fast.

The fat white snail emerged from the shadows. His red, white, and blue shell was way too small for his body, and a little toy bee dangled off the back of it. He wore round sunglasses that made him look like a biker.

"Here one second, gone the next. They call me the White Shadow, 'cause I'm so fast all you see is my shadow," he said.

"I don't get it," Turbo said.

"I'm fast. Like a shadow," White Shadow explained.

"Yeah, but shadows, they're not inherently fast," Turbo argued.

White Shadow backed up into the shadows and disappeared . . . sort of. It was hard for the big, white snail to disappear anywhere.

"White Shadooooow," he said mysteriously.

"I can still see you," Turbo said.

Whiplash inched up next to Turbo. "Listen, garden snail, I'm here to invite you to join our crew," Whiplash said.

Turbo tried not to laugh. "Join your crew?"

Whiplash scowled. "Did I say something humorous?"

"I'm sorry," Turbo replied. "It's just that . . . you guys are, you know, kinda slow."

The racing snails suddenly looked angry.

"Oh really?" Skidmark asked.

Panicked, Chet pulled Turbo aside. "What are you doing?"

"Now I'm gonna pretend I didn't hear what I *clearly* just heard," Whiplash said, glaring at Turbo.

"Heard what?" Chet asked with a nervous laugh. "I didn't hear anything. Nothing out of order."

Turbo looked Whiplash in the eyes. "Oh, I meant what I said."

"Enough talk!" Whiplash boomed. He looked around the taco shop with a dramatic gleam in his eye. "It's time for . . . action!"

A few minutes later, all the snails were back in the parking lot, lined up in front of the auto body shop, ready to race.

"It's simple," Whiplash said. He nodded up to the STARLIGHT PLAZA sign. "First one to the top of that shooting star wins."

Turbo followed his gaze to the blinking neon star on top of the sign. He smirked in amusement.

"You guys? Way up there, huh?" he asked. "Awesome. Hold on. Let me get out my calendar . . . so I can time you."

Skidmark got right in his face. "Oh, you got jokes, rookie?"

"Laugh it up, garden snail," Whiplash warned.

Then Whiplash, Burn, Smoove Move, and Skidmark shuffled onto a piece of plywood and lined up. Turbo didn't know what they were up to, but he wasn't worried.

"On your mark . . . ," began Burn.

"Get yo' self set . . . ," said Smoove Move.

"And prepare to be . . . White Shadowed!"

Turbo looked up to see White Shadow on top of a telephone pole. He jumped off the pole, landing on the end of the plywood plank, opposite the other snails.

Wham! He catapulted the four snails into the air.

"Whoa!" Turbo cried.

The snails latched on to a cable. Smoove Move used an ice-pop stick like a snowboard, and the four of them slid down the line, headed right for the star. The race was on!

"Those guys are crazy!" Chet said, trembling at the thought of being up so high.

"Those guys are *awesome!*" Turbo corrected him.

He took off like a shot across the parking lot, leaving a blue streak in his wake.

"Hey, player!" Smoove Move called down. "The party is up here!"

Turbo raced across the parking lot.

"How do I get up there?" he wondered.

He sprinted up the side of the taco stand and scooted onto another cable leading toward the star. It wasn't easy to keep his balance, but his speed helped push him forward.

Zoom! He passed Skidmark . . . and Burn . . . and Smoove Move . . . and finally, Whiplash.

"Later!" Turbo said as he scooted past.

His triumphant smile faded when he saw that the wire ended at a utility pole. He stopped himself as quickly as he could.

But the racing snails did the opposite. They sped

up, using the utility pole like a ramp to launch themselves onto the star. They soared through the air.
Whiplash landed first, followed by the others.

Whiplash looked over at Turbo, who was still on
the utility pole, and flashed him a smug grin.

"Who's slow-ish now, garden snail?" he asked.

Turbo grinned back. His new friends were awesome!

Destined for Greatness

Turbo had never been happier. Thanks to the freak encounter with the race car, he had superspeed. He had new friends who understood his love of racing. At night, though, he still dreamed of racing in the Indy 500, but Turbo knew that was only a dream.

Tito had a dream too—to make Dos Bros Tacos a success. The next morning he placed Turbo on the brim of his yellow cap and climbed up on the billboard in front of the strip mall. He carefully painted a banner on it: SEE THE WORLD'S FASTEST SNAIL WHILE EATING THE WORLD'S BEST TACOS!

Angelo came out of the shop, carrying the trash.

"What are you doing?" he asked, looking up at the billboard.

"Planning a taco-volution!" Tito replied. "It's a little concept that I came up with when you combine the words—"

"Taco and revolution. I get it," Angelo said drily. "But how's that supposed to help us sell tacos?"

"Patience, bro," Tito said. "Taco-volutions don't happen in a day."

Angelo sighed and went back into the restaurant. Tito sat on the edge of the billboard and looked down at the road, hopefully waiting for customers to drive by, see the sign, and pull into the strip mall.

He and Turbo waited . . . and waited . . . and waited. Nobody came into Bobby's hobby shop or Kim-Ly's nail salon or Paz's garage, either.

As the sun set on the strip mall, Tito finally gave up. He climbed down from the billboard and went back to the taco stand. He didn't need to say anything. Angelo nodded and handed him a taco, and the two brothers ate in silence.

Turbo headed outside to get a better look at his new home. As he sat on the hood of the taco truck, Chet crawled up next to him.

"Listen up," he said. "I think I've got the solution. All we have to do is find that same car you fell on the other night, you following me? Stuff you back inside the engine, and *run it in reverse*."

"Okay, that's insane," Turbo told him.

Chet ignored him. "Then we can go back home, and pretend like none of this ever happened!"

"Or, maybe getting fired from the plant was a good thing," Turbo said cautiously. He knew his brother didn't feel the same way he did.

Chet wiggled his eyestalks furiously. "A *good* thing? A *good* thing?"

"Yeah, look at that," Turbo replied, nodding up toward the roof of the taco stand.

The racing snails were riding paper airplanes off the roof. They glided on the breeze.

"Hi, Chet!" Burn called out.

"You just witnessed snails having *fun*," Turbo pointed out. "Don't you think that's great?"

"We don't belong here," Chet insisted.

Turbo chuckled to himself. "Yeah, well, that's exactly how I felt every day back in that garden."

"Okay, so what's your plan, then?" Chet challenged him. "Stay here in this run-down strip mall with a bunch of lunatic snails and a nutso taco man who is using you to sell Mexican food? Because if that's your plan then whoopty-skippy-do, sign me up!"

Tito appeared, leaning over the hood.

"My ears are burning. I hope you're not talking about me," he joked. Of course, he had no idea that the snails really could talk to each other.

"You two seem to have a special connection, little amigo and Snail Who Seems to Be Friends with Little Amigo," he said, leaning closer. "Is this your mother? Your sister? Oh, say no more. It's your girlfriend!"

Tito playfully tickled Chet's chin.

"Ah, she's a cutie," Tito said.

Annoyed, Chet chomped down on Tito's finger.

"Ow!" Tito yelled, shaking his head. "Women."

Tito leaned against the hood of the car and talked to Turbo. "I have to admit, I was kind of hoping the taco-volution would've started by now," he said. "With my brains and your speed we should be destined for greatness, right?"

Turbo looked up at Tito with wide eyes. *Yes! Yes!* Turbo thought.

"We need to think big, little amigo," Tito said. "I'm talking commercials, talk shows, county fairs. Flea markets, farmers' markets, supermarkets—we'll cover *all* the markets!"

A delivery truck screeched to a stop in front of the strip mall. The side of the truck had a huge image of Guy Gagné holding up a bottle of Adrenalode Energy Drink. The words PROUD SPONSOR OF THE INDY 500 were emblazoned underneath him.

Turbo's eyes locked on the truck. The Indy 500! Of course! If they entered the Indy 500, the taco stand would get lots of publicity, and Turbo could achieve his dream.

He looked at Tito, but Tito wasn't looking at the truck. Panicked, Turbo zipped to the street and up the side of the truck. He circled the words Indy 500, and as he went faster and faster, a bright blue light surrounded it.

Later, Turbo zipped around the taco-stand counter, circling Chet as Tito talked to his brother inside.

"I want to enter the snail in the Indy 500," he announced.

"The Indy 500? What are you talking about?" Angelo asked.

"Now I know it sounds crazy . . . ," Tito began.

"This is way beyond crazy," Angelo said.

Tito took a booklet from his pocket—the official rule book of the Indy 500.

"Actually, I've been doing some research," Tito said. "There's nothing in the rules that says a snail can't enter the race."

Angelo picked up a sponge by the sink. "There's nothing that says this sponge can't enter the race either, but that doesn't mean it's ever gonna happen."

"*Millions* of people watch that race!" Tito pointed out. "This could put us on the map, bro!"

Angelo flipped a tortilla on the grill. "I'm trying to work here."

Tito grabbed a tortilla warmer marked New Oven Fund

from a nearby shelf. He opened it, pulling out a wad of cash.

"Come on, Angelo. All we have to do is raise the twenty thousand dollar registration fee," Tito pleaded. "And I figured that once we sell the truck . . ."

"Sell the truck? Are you even listening to yourself, Tito?" Angelo asked. "You want to invest our entire life savings in a snail."

He snatched the tortilla warmer from Tito's hands and then placed it on the shelf.

Tito gazed out the window at the STARLIGHT PLAZA sign. "I'm telling you, this snail crawled into our lives for a reason," he said dreamily. "I think he could be our little shooting star."

Turbo had never felt more proud in his life. "Did you hear that, Chet? This guy believes in me."

"That guy is as crazy as you are," Chet snorted.

Angelo walked off, and Chet followed him. Turbo looked up at Tito and revved his shell. Tito heard the noise and looked down at the snail, smiling.

"Don't worry, little amigo," he said. "We'll get that registration fee somehow."

Don't Screw This Up!

Like Turbo, Tito was a dreamer, and he wasn't going to give up on this dream. All of the Indy 500 drivers had sponsors, didn't they? He could get sponsors too. But when he asked everyone to chip in for the registration fee, they weren't interested.

Tito slumped against the wall of Paz's garage, defeated. Turbo crawled up next to him just as a bus full of tourists was driving by the Starlight Plaza. The racing snails were ready for them.

"All right, team," Whiplash says. "Time to *snail up!*"

Splat! White Shadow jumped onto the windshield right in front of the tour bus driver's face. He swerved the vehicle, momentarily startled. At the same time,

Skidmark knocked over several glass bottles from the taco stand's trash bin. The bus's tires rolled over the broken glass.

At this point Whiplash turned to Turbo. "Light her up, Turbo! Do your thing, baby!"

Turbo immediately circling the billboard advertising the world's fastest snail, lighting the sign with glowing blue light.

All the tourists piled out of the bus, curious.

"Hey, Angelo, we got customers!" Tito shouted.

While Paz fixed the bus, the tourists feasted on tacos and watched Turbo win an amazing snail race. Before they left, the women had their nails done at Kim-Ly's nail salon, and the men shopped in Bobby's Hobby Store. Everyone had a great time.

As they left, the bus driver leaned out the window and said to Tito, "Good luck with that snail of yours!"

Tito smiled and waved. "Thank you, my friend!"

At the end of the day, Angelo happily counted up the money in the register.

"I gotta hand it to you, Tito," Angelo admitted. "For once, one of your crazy schemes worked. We sold over ten percent more tacos today!"

Angelo put some money in the tortilla warmer and then picked up a garbage bag to take outside. Tito followed him, excited.

"I know," he said. "And, hey, if we did ten percent better because of that billboard, just imagine what the Indy 500 could do!"

Angelo's smile faded. "Hey, don't go crazy on me. We had a good day. We sold a few extra tacos. It's good enough."

Sighing, Tito placed Turbo on a table next to the racing snails. Why didn't anyone believe in him?

Then Paz, Bobby, and Kim-Ly walked over, and Paz slapped an envelope full of money on the counter.

"You better not screw this up, Tito," Paz said firmly.

Tito and Turbo slowly began to smile, and the other snails danced around Chet.

"We're going to Indianapolis!" they cheered.

Chet groaned, wondering when this nightmare would end. But Turbo was grinning.

His dream was just beginning.

Turbo's New Look

The next morning the taco truck zipped down the highway, taking the long road from Van Nuys, California, to Indianapolis, Indiana. Tito was at the wheel, ignoring the constant cell phone calls from Angelo. He knew his brother would be upset when he found out he used their savings to make up the rest of the registration fee, but he hoped Angelo would forgive him once they were famous.

But they still had miles to go. The snails hung out in the back of the truck, watching as Bobby, Kim-Ly, and Paz tried to come up with a racing name for Turbo. They didn't know he had one already.

"Bullet?"

"Rocket?"

"Blaze?"

But nothing seemed right, and the snails decided to give them a little hint. They inched up to the moon roof on the back of the truck and spelled out "T-U-R-B-O" with their bodies. They cast a shadow right onto Bobby's notebook.

"That's it! Turbo!" Tito yelled, and the others nodded in agreement.

The next day they got to work customizing Turbo's shell. The old decals came off, and Kim-Ly carefully painted it a new shiny blue with red and white swirls. Then she added a black number five on a white background. Bobby added vents on either side of the shell.

After miles and miles, they finally saw a sign on the highway.

WELCOME TO INDIANAPOLIS! HOME OF THE INDY 500!

Turbo stared in awe as they drove up to the famous speedway. A massive archway flanked by black-and-white-checked columns that looked like racing flags welcomed visitors. The top part of the arch read INDIANAPOLIS MOTOR SPEEDWAY. Turbo had seen the image on TV before, but now they were really here! He could hardly believe it. He was bursting with excitement.

Tito parked the truck, and the snails piled on a plastic take-out tray so that Bobby could carry them around. The place bustled with activity—fans milled around, hoping to spot their favorite racers, and haulers delivered shiny Indy cars covered with sponsor logos. They passed groups of reporters and news cameras as they made their way to Gasoline Alley, the row of garages where all the cars were kept. Turbo looked up at the sign, awestruck.

I can't believe I'm really here! he thought.

Then he heard it—the loud roar of a familiar engine. He turned his head to see a red blur racing past on the track.

"Guy Gagné," he whispered.

Transfixed, he scooted up to the scoring tower to get a better view. Guy's sleek car had a long thin nose and the black Adrenalode logo on the side. Turbo watched the display board that clocked the time for every lap Guy took around the two-and-a-half-mile track.

Onlookers shuddered from the speed as Guy made his last blistering lap around the track.

FOUR LAP AVERAGE: 230 MPH

"That's Guy's best time yet," Turbo realized.

Down on the ground, Tito frowned. "Turbo's never gone that fast," he whispered.

Kim-Ly glared at him. "So, you got a plan, Taco Man? We're waiting."

"Of course I do," Tito said. He took a pair of eyeglasses from his pocket and put them on.

Paz shook her head. "Please tell me those phony glasses are not your plan."

"Uh, no, that's not my plan. That would be ridiculous," he replied. But as he walked away, he mumbled, "Come on, phony glasses, do your thing."

Turbo zipped down from the scoring tower and slid into Tito's shirt pocket as Tito marched up to the registration office. He confidently slapped down the wad of money at the counter in front of an overworked-looking official.

"I have a driver that I'd like to enter in the race," Tito said.

"What team does your driver race for?" the official asked in a bored monotone.

"Dos Bros Tacos and Company!" Tito said proudly.

The official skeptically eyed Tito. "Has he passed the Rookie Test?"

Tito leaned in closer. "Hey, let's cut to the chase. You have glasses; I have glasses. What do we gotta do to get this done, bro?"

Tito exited the registration office moments later— escorted by two security guards. Bobby, Kim-Ly, and Paz shook their heads in disappointment.

At that moment Guy Gagné pulled up right in front of them in his race car, and a horde of fans and reporters quickly gathered around.

"Guy, how do you do it, shattering your own records year after year?" one of the reporters asked him.

Guy's chest puffed up a little as he answered. "Well, when a cheetah chases after a gazelle, does he ever stop to think, maybe I've caught enough gazelles? Maybe I should just settle down, try the vegan thing? No! He keeps running as long as his legs will carry him. I am like the cheetah. I will never give up. Next question!"

Bobby wasn't interested. "All right, Tito, give me the keys. I'll drive the first shift home."

But Turbo was inspired. He revved his engine, jerking Tito forward.

"Whoa! What gives?" Tito asked.

Turbo revved again, harder this time, pulling Tito toward Guy Gagné. He dragged Tito through the mob of reporters and up and over the racetrack wall. Tito collapsed in a heap at Guy's feet.

"Can I help you, *monsieur*?" Guy asked, clearly annoyed.

Tito looked up at him sheepishly. "One second, please."

As Turbo crawled out of his pocket, Tito hissed, "Are you trying to get me arrested?"

But Turbo nodded toward the track's starting line. Tito nodded, understanding, just as the registration official ran up, out of breath. Tito knew what he had to do.

"Ladies and gentlemen, I give you the next Indy 500 champion!" he announced. Then he held Turbo up for all to see.

Guy squinted. "Is that a *snail*?"

People in the crowd started to laugh.

"What kind of welcome is that?" Whiplash asked from his perch on the tray.

"I'd say an appropriate reaction, given the situation," Chet said smugly.

Two security guards grabbed Tito, and Whiplash grinned at Chet.

"Have a nice flight," Whiplash said.

Before Chet could ask what that meant, White Shadow jumped off Bobby's shoulder and onto the tray, launching Chet and the other racing snails into the air. They landed on the faces of the guards, who screamed, trying to shake them off. With the guards distracted, Tito placed Turbo on the starting line.

"Go!" Tito yelled.

Zoom! Turbo whipped around the track as fast as his shell could take him . . . lapping the track once . . . twice . . . three times . . . four times. . . .

A boy in the crowd filmed Turbo with his cell phone.

"Whoa . . . that snail is fast!" he remarked.

Turbo screeched to a stop next to Tito. They eagerly checked out the display board.

"That's enough to qualify!" Whiplash yelled.

"That's what I'm talking about!" Tito cried, picking up Turbo. Then he turned around to see the spectators—the reporters, the racing official, the fans, and even Guy Gagné—frozen in disbelief.

Then they all burst into excited chatter. Had they really seen that?

The kid with the cell phone uploaded the video of Turbo to the Internet.

"Oh man, wait'll people see this . . ."

Let the Snail Race!

All over the world the video of Turbo speeding around the track popped up on cell phones and computers. Everyone kept sharing the unbelievable footage.

Back at the strip mall, Angelo was busy replacing the "Dos Bros" part of the taco sign, (which meant "Two Brothers") with the words "Uno Bros," (which meant "One Brother"). He knew it didn't make much sense, but he was so angry and he was done with Tito and his crazy schemes.

Then he looked down—and saw a long line of customers behind him. Angelo put down the sign. Had Tito's plan actually worked this time?

The Turbo video even made it to the man in

charge of the Indy 500, the CEO. He was pulling into the speedway when his cell phone rang.

"Have you heard?" asked a voice at the other end. "That snail is fast."

"Yes, I've heard," the CEO replied. "Forget about it. It'll blow over fast."

The CEO made his way to the boardroom where a wall of TVs was blaring news of the amazing snail on twelve different stations.

"You cannot enter a snail in the Indy 500!" argued one news anchor.

"Others feel that the snail could be crushed by the giant race cars . . . ," a second reporter was saying.

And a third cheered, "It will be the single most anticipated sporting event in all of history!"

The CEO frowned. What was he supposed to do about this mess? It certainly wasn't going to blow over by lunchtime. It looked like he was going to have to hold a press conference.

Reporters crowded the pressroom, scrambling to get sound bites from the Indy drivers as they entered.

Outside, the racing fans watched the action on a Jumbotron. Everyone was eager to find out what the CEO would do about the fast little snail called Turbo.

Tito entered, holding Turbo, and the reporters raced to them. Guy Gagné frowned as the reporters stopped interviewing him. Then the CEO walked in, nervously adjusting his tie, and everyone got quiet.

"After careful consideration, I've decided that I simply cannot permit a snail to enter—"

Panicked, Tito stood up. "Please, sir, give my snail a shot, and I swear you won't regret it!" he pleaded.

The reporters looked at the CEO. Would he change his mind?

"Mr. Lopez, while I appreciate your enthusiasm, my decision is—" he began, but Kim-Ly, Bobby, and Paz interrupted him.

"Let him race! Let him race! Let him race!" they chanted.

"Now, now. Order," the CEO said, looking highly uncomfortable.

To everyone's surprise, Guy put an arm around Tito and looked right into one of the news cameras.

"I, like this passionate gentleman here, came from humble beginnings. In the words of my dear father, no dream is too big, and no dreamer too small."

Turbo looked up at his hero in awe. Guy was standing up for him!

"And that is why I, for one, believe that if the Indy 500 isn't going to put a limit on speed, it shouldn't put a limit on spirit!" Guy said. "Give the people what they want! Let him race!"

The chant spread throughout the pressroom, and soon all the fans watching on the Jumbotron joined in. The chant seemed to rock the entire speedway.

It was too much for the CEO. "All right!" he yelled.

Everyone got quiet. "All right . . . what?" Tito asked.

The CEO took a deep breath. "Your snail can compete in the Indianapolis 500."

The crowd exploded in stunned and happy cheers. Tito jumped up and down, waving Turbo in the air. Bobby, Kim-Ly, and Paz hugged one another. Next to them the racing snails did happy backflips and high fives. Only Chet looked miserable.

"Has the world lost its mind?" he wondered.

The next few hours were a whirlwind for Turbo, Tito, and their friends. Every reporter wanted to talk to them, and every fan wanted an autograph. After a while they retreated to the taco truck where they watched themselves on the news.

Tito was sobbing to one of the reporters like he had just won a beauty contest. "I'm just soooo happy."

"And we'd be happy to see you come on down to the Starlight Plaza," Bobby added, getting into the frame.

Paz jumped in. "Just north of the 101 freeway in Van Nuys, California!"

Back in the taco truck the shop owners were all

grinning. This was going to be great for business!

The racing snails slept in the drawer of the cash register while Turbo sat on the shelf above them, still awake.

Tito came by to give him a kiss. "Sleep tight, little amigo. We've got a big day tomorrow."

Then Turbo heard his brother's voice. "Yup. 'Big day' indeed."

Turbo looked up and saw Chet sitting by a bag of tomatoes on a nearby shelf.

"I'm detecting a refreshing note of disapproval in your voice," Turbo said.

"I'm worried," Chet said.

"I'll be fine," Turbo insisted.

"You are delusional, you know that?" Chet said. "It's Big Red all over again. Only this time instead of one lawn mower, it'll be thirty-two giant fire-breathing cars. And I won't be able to save you."

"You won't have to," Turbo shot back, "because this time, I have *speed*."

"You're not a car. You're a snail," Chet reminded him. "Welcome to reality!"

"Oh yeah? Can a snail do this?" Turbo asked. He flicked on his highlights, blinding Chet.

Chet shook his head. "I'm begging you, please, just quit while you are ahead!"

"This is happening, Chet," Turbo said firmly.

"But Theo—"

"You know what? My name is Turbo," Turbo said, his voice rising. "I've wanted this my whole life. All these people, they believe in me. . . . Why won't you?"

Turbo zipped out of the truck, hurt and angry. He headed out to Gasoline Alley, still turning over Chet's words in his head. Why couldn't his brother just be happy for him, for once?

Then a sliver of light coming from one of the garages caught his eye. He snuck in through a crack in the door and found himself staring right at Guy Gagné's legendary race car.

He sighed happily. "I think I'm in love."

Looking up, he saw a shelf containing all five of Guy's Indy 500 trophies. He zipped over to the shiny treasures and climbed up on one.

"You're not trying to steal my trophy now, are you?"

Turbo whirled around to see Guy Gagné standing behind him!

"Because if you want one for yourself, you may have a long wait," Guy told him.

Turbo nodded awestruck.

Guy fixed himself a steaming beverage from a machine. He turned to stare at Turbo.

"So," Guy went on, "you are my *little* competition, eh? The underdog versus the champion. The world loves the underdogs, you know. The dreamers out there, they need them. Need to believe that one day, maybe they could achieve the impossible too."

Turbo smiled. Guy knew exactly how he felt.

Then Guy eyed Turbo, and his dark eyes gleamed with a look that wasn't friendly. "Well, the sad truth is, underdogs seldom win. And dreamers? Let's just say, eventually they have to wake up."

Turbo looked at Guy, confused. What was he saying? This wasn't the wonderful Guy Gagné he had admired his whole life.

Guy picked up Turbo. "I've never talked to a snail before. So small . . . so amusing. No wonder they want to see you race!"

Holding Turbo by the shell, Guy moved him around the air in circles, like he was going around a racetrack.

"*Vroom! Vroom!* Ha! Look at him go!"

Guy walked to the garage door and placed Turbo back on the ground.

"Crawl home, garden snail," he said, "while you still can."

Then he slammed the door shut. Turbo stood there for a moment, stunned.

Everything he had ever wanted to be, and everything he had become, was because of Guy.

But Guy didn't mean any of it. It was all a lie. Did that mean Chet was right? That Turbo was just kidding himself?

He slowly inched back to the taco truck, his confidence shaken.

Start Your Engines!

"Goooood afternoon, race fans, and welcome to this year's running of the Indianapolis 500!"

The entire speedway buzzed with excitement as the starting time for the race grew closer. Pit crews wheeled the glistening Indy cars out of Gasoline Alley and onto the track. More than 350,000 spectators filled the stands, watching as the cars rolled into their poll positions. Skywriting planes circled overhead, and fireworks exploded in the blue sky.

The taco truck stayed parked in the parking lot, and Turbo sat on the counter as curious fans and reporters gathered around to snap pictures of him. Others passed by, calling out words of encouragement.

"Good luck out there!"

"Hope you don't get run over!"

Both Turbo and Tito were pretty nervous, but they knew there was no backing out now. Tito shooed away the fans, and he ordered the shopkeepers to board the truck.

"Everybody in! It's go time!"

As the truck took off toward the starting gate, Chet watched from a picnic table. He didn't plan on watching the race.

"Be careful out there, Theo," he said sadly.

Then out of nowhere, a hand scooped Chet off the table! Horrified, Chet looked up into the face of an eight-year-old boy named Danny.

"Hey, little snail, are you lost?" Danny asked.

"No," Chet replied, but of course the boy couldn't hear him. He held Chet by the shell and pretended to make him fly through the air.

"Are you a boy or a girl? Blast off!" Danny cried, and then he took off running.

"Put me down!" Chet wailed.

The boy carried Chet up to a deluxe VIP skybox

and placed him on the armrest of a leather chair.

"Here you go, little snail! Now you've got the best seat in the house!" Danny said happily.

Chet groaned. Through the window in front of him he had a perfect view of the racetrack, as well as the fans, the cars, and the huge image of his brother that had just popped up on the giant TV screen.

"This isn't happening," Chet said, panicking. He started to inch away, but the boy placed a small drinking glass over him.

"Stay here. I'll be right back!" the boy said and then ran off.

"Help! Let me out!" he cried.

It looked like he was going to see the race, whether he wanted to or not. And so far, things weren't great for Turbo. The announcers started to make fun of Tito as he pulled the taco truck up to the track.

"You know, food trucks are very popular these days. And I do love a good taco," one of them said.

Tito smiled and waved at the crowd, and then he placed Turbo on the starting line. Turbo nervously gazed up at the monstrous cars on either side of them. He felt smaller than he'd ever felt in his life.

The CEO stepped up to a microphone. "Good afternoon and welcome to what has become the most anticipated and unprecedented running of the Indianapolis 500. So without further ado . . . ladies and gentlemen . . . and snail . . . start your engines!"

Cylinders pounded as the cars roared to life, shooting hot flames from their exhaust pipes. The ground underneath Turbo rumbled from the vibrations.

Behind Turbo, the racing snails bounced up and down.

"See ya in the winner's circle, garden snail!" Whiplash called out as loud as he could.

Tito leaned down to Turbo. "Everything's gonna be fine, okay?" he said. "We can do this, right?"

Turbo gamely revved his engine. He might be nervous, but he wasn't going to let Tito down. Not now. Not *ever* if he could help it.

Tito's eyes welled with tears. "Oh, I wish I was tiny so I could give you a hug," he said.

"Get off the track!" the official yelled.

"Okay! Okay! I'm going!" Tito said, and he

jogged off the track. "Good luck out there, Turbo!"

Turbo revved his engine as the pace car rolled onto the track. To start the race, the cars would follow the pace car in a slow parade lap a few times around the track. Tito, his friends, and the racing snails watched the laps from the pit. Up in the VIP booth, Chet turned his head—he couldn't bear to look.

"The pace car is off and the parade laps are underway. Only moments until the green flag drops and history is made here at Indianapolis!" the announcer crowed.

At the end of the final pace lap, Turbo took a deep breath.

"Let's do this," he told himself as he crossed the starting line.

The green flag dropped, and the racers blasted into high gear, grinding pedals against metal as they exploded off the line. Cars flew past Turbo with tires the size of steamrollers. Their motion sent Turbo thrashing, and he nearly flew off the track.

"Turbo's struggling out there!" said the announcer. "I've seen better performances at my six-year-old's piano recital, and he is not very good!"

Turbo just couldn't get in the game. He felt over-whelmed by the noise and the dust coughed up by every car that passed him. For the first time he felt he was just too tiny for this. Even the grooves in the track—which were nothing for the race cars—were a huge challenge for him.

"He's getting killed out there!" Bobby cried.

Paz looked upset. "What have we done?"

On the track Guy Gagné looked in his rearview and chuckled at the sight of the struggling snail. Then he pulled into his pit stop, and his crew expertly changed his tires and refueled him in seconds before sending him back on the track.

Turbo was the last to get to his pit stop.

"All right! Go! Go! Go!" Tito yelled.

Bobby, Kim-Ly, and Paz all tripped over one another trying to get to the tiny snail. Whiplash shook his head.

"That's it. This pit crew is officially under new management," Whiplash said.

White Shadow bounced onto the tray again,

launching the snails onto the ground next to Turbo. Whiplash began barking out commands.

"Air jack!"

"Jack-tivate!" Smoove Move responded. He hoisted Turbo off the ground and flipped him upside down.

"Lube!"

"Applied liberally," Skidmark replied, applying slippery lip balm to Turbo's foot.

"Detailing!"

"Wax on, wax off!" Burn cried. She slapped a piece of sticky tape onto Turbo's face and then quickly pulled it off, along with a bunch of dirt and soot.

"Fuel!"

Whiplash jammed a giant bottle of water down Turbo's throat. "Down the hatch! Chug! Chug! Chug!"

"Foot massage!"

"You know it!" Burn said. She turned on the vibrate setting of a cell phone, and put Turbo on top. His whole body jiggled as the phone shook.

"Relaxing vibes!" Whiplash ordered next.

"On it, brother," Smoove Move said. He slapped

headphones on Turbo, blasting the smooth sounds of a saxophone.

"Now *de*-lax those vibes!"

Smoove Move nodded, changing the music to superloud heavy metal. Turbo whipped off the headphones.

"Are you crazy?" he asked.

Whiplash slapped him across the face. "Yeah, I'm crazy! What made you think I was sane?" he yelled like a charged-up drill sergeant.

"Listen, I can't drive in—"

Whiplash slapped him again.

"Are you a car?" he asked.

"No," Turbo replied.

"Are. You. A. Car?" Whiplash yelled.

"No!" Turbo yelled back.

"Then stop driving like one," Whiplash said.

Turbo started to rev up as the advice sank in. Of course. He was a tiny snail, not a massive race car.

"Now get out there," Whiplash said. "Snail up, baby!"

Turbo Snails Up

"Gagné with a commanding lead now, followed by Claudio Cruz, Shelby Stone, and Takao Noguchi," the announcer informed the crowd.

Turbo ramped up to full speed as he got back into the race. He knew what Whiplash wanted him to do—as a snail he could have advantages on the track that the other cars didn't. But he needed to figure out how to do that—and fast.

He zipped along the track, passing two cars. But when he tried to pass a third, the car slid in front of him, blocking him.

"No. Come on," Turbo muttered.

For the first time he noticed the narrow space

under the car in front of him. It was risky, but it was the only shot he had.

"Snail up!" Turbo cried.

Zoom! He sped underneath the car, leaning forward to avoid grazing his head on the car's violently shaking underside. One false move and he'd be toast.

Snail up! he told himself, willing himself forward. Finally he saw the light at the other end of the car. He zipped out from under the front wing. He'd made it!

"I don't believe it! Turbo just went *under* a car!" the announcer cried.

In the VIP booth Chet looked over his shoulder with one eyeball. It was true! Heartened, he turned both eyeballs toward the screen.

Turbo was feeling more confident too. He realized he was small enough that he could go between two cars and pass them, turning on his headlights so he could avoid obstacles.

"Despite a rocky start, it looks like Turbo is gaining some ground," the announcer said in disbelief.

"Yeah! Now we're talking!" Whiplash cheered from the pit.

Determined to get to the front of the pack, Turbo passed under three more cars. He zoomed out from under the third and set his sights on the next car in front of him.

The driver, Takao Noguchi, saw Turbo in his mirror. His expression hardened as he steered left and right, trying to make it impossible for Turbo to safely pass underneath him. As he made the turn, his car practically hugged the wall. Grinning, Takao looked in the mirror again, but he couldn't see Turbo anywhere.

His smile faded as he started to panic. "Where is he? Where is he?"

From the corner of his eye he saw a familiar blue light reflecting off his helmet. Turning right, he saw Turbo racing on the side of the wall!

Turbo sped along the wall, easily overtaking Takao and zooming back onto the track. The crowd exploded in wild cheers.

"He passed another one!" Tito yelled.

Still stuck inside the glass in the VIP booth, Chet cheered his brother on.

"Go! Go! Go! Left turn! Left turn! Left turn!"

Down below, Turbo rocketed his way into third place. He eyed the second-place car, driven by Shelby Stone, as it took the turn.

Bam! Stone accidentally took the turn too wide, grazing the wall. One of his tires popped off and went flying backward—aimed right at Turbo!

With no time to think, Turbo leaped into the air, flying right through the center of the tire! He landed back on the track, beaming with confidence.

"Turbo maneuvers past Shelby Stone and into second place!" the first announcer reported.

"He is hot on Gagné's heels!" observed the second announcer.

The crowd rose to their feet, clapping and calling Turbo's name.

Nothing bothered Guy Gagné more than that. For years he had been the star of the Indy 500, and now some snail was stealing his spotlight.

Turbo tried to come up on Guy's left, but the racer cut him off. Turbo banked around to the other side to attempt a pass on the right.

Up ahead Turbo saw they were about to pass two

cars that they had already lapped. The cars banked around a turn, but one took the turn high and grazed a patch of black, rubber tire bits that had accumulated on the track during the race. The car swerved wildly, but the driver recovered.

"These racers better watch it coming into turn four," the announcer commented. "This late in the race, that outside edge is full of marbles. And you don't want to play with *these* marbles, kids. That rubber peeling off the tires can be a minefield for these drivers!"

Gagné's annoyed expression brightened as he spotted the rubber marbles on the turn up ahead. He had an idea.

"Here we go," he muttered.

He pushed to the right, forcing Turbo toward the outer edge of the track by the wall. Suddenly a big chunk of rubber came flying at Turbo. He dodged it, bewildered.

Looking ahead, he saw a sea of rubber marbles littering the track. He knew that for a full-size car, the debris could be slippery. But for Turbo, it was like navigating an obstacle course through a field of boulders. If he hit just one of them at the high speed he was traveling, the force would send him tumbling off the track.

Turbo zigzagged around the marbles, desperately trying to get back to the inside of the track, but Guy's car blocked him in. To make things worse, Guy steered his car slightly to the right, kicking marbles up into the air. A meteor shower of the rubber bits fell on Turbo, and he frantically ducked and dodged his way out of them.

Then one of the marbles hit his shell, causing him to lose control. He smacked against the wall—and then he heard a sickening crack.

Shaken, Turbo steadied himself and made his way toward the pit. Something was wrong—really wrong.

"Turbo!" Tito cried in alarm.

Pileup!

Turbo's vision blurred as the pit crew examined him. As he slowly regained focus, he saw Tito staring at the back of his shell with concern. Turbo stretched his eyestalk to look—and almost passed out. A large crack spiderwebbed across his shell, leaking blue fluid. His vision went blurry again. After a while he heard his friends talking.

"What are we gonna do?" Bobby asked. "If he takes another hit like that one . . ."

"You have to pull him, Tito," Paz said.

Tito turned to Turbo, heartbroken.

"I'm sorry, little amigo. It's over," Tito said.

Turbo was confused. What happened to never

giving up? Did Tito really believe it was over?

Then he heard the familiar roar of an engine and turned an eye to see Guy's red race car pulling out of the pit. In Turbo's haze the car morphed into Big Red, the tomato back home.

Something clicked inside of Turbo. His engine revved, and his vision came back into focus.

"Not yet," Turbo said.

Whoosh! Before Tito could stop him, Turbo burst from the pit at top speed. He blasted back onto the track, his shell dangerously sputtering blue fluid.

"With the green flag about to be waved, it looks like a mere formality at this point," the announcer was saying. "Guy Gagné is just five laps away from victory."

Zoom! A blazing blue light rocketed back onto the scene.

"Wait a minute! Turbo is still in this thing!" the announcer crowed.

The green flag waved, and the cars on the track revved up to full speed. Turbo surged back into the action just in time to take second place behind Guy once more.

Now Guy wasn't just annoyed—he was furious! Turbo had a clear path right underneath Guy's car. He zoomed forward . . .

Suddenly the blue light in Turbo's shell went out! Turbo shot backward like a missile, screaming.

When he landed on the track, the blue light flashed on again, and Turbo zipped ahead. Once again he got into position right behind Guy, ready to move underneath. And once again his power conked out!

"Theo!" Chet yelled from the VIP box.

Stalled on the track, Turbo started to imagine things. The cars around him turned into tomatoes. The slick track became a grassy lawn. The car behind him was a lawn mower, about to shred him to pieces.

Turbo flicked his shell with his tail, willing the light and his superspeed to come back on. A car loomed behind him, about to crush him, when Turbo's shell powered back on.

He jetted forward, and everything came back into focus. The tomatoes turned back into cars, the grass turned back into asphalt. He had faced his worst fears—and triumphed this time.

That confidence spurred him onward. He kept Guy in his sights.

"Come on, just hold in there a little longer," Turbo urged, looking back at his shell.

He caught up to Guy again, squeezing between his car and the wall.

"No!" Guy yelled. He inched closer to the wall, pushing Turbo into the cement. His shell sparked as it scraped against the concrete. Any more pressure from Guy, and he'd be crushed.

Once again Turbo had to think like a snail. Just before he could be squashed, he hopped into the wheel well of Guy's car. Once Guy pulled away from the wall, he hopped off and rocketed up to one of the fence poles. Then like his friends the racing snails had taught him, he launched himself into the air.

He soared past Guy's windshield, and Guy stared at him, stunned. Then Turbo landed on the track right in front of Guy.

"Unbelievable! Turbo is in the lead!" the announcer declared.

The crowd went wild, and then a white flag waved

over the finish line. Everyone in the stadium cheered.

"And the white flag's in the air as we enter the two hundredth and final lap!" the announcer reported.

Guy and Turbo came around the final turn, weaving through the cars they had already lapped. Guy pushed his car to the limits, driving like he never had before. He frowned when he saw Turbo easily pass through the narrow opening between two cars ahead.

Determined to pass Turbo, Guy had to drive high on the wall—and right into the rubber marbles. He tightened his grip on the wheel and banked hard.

"Guy's in the marbles!" the announcer observed.

Weaving through the stretch of slippery rubber, Guy struggled to keep control of his car.

His crew chief's voice came through his headphones. "Guy, what are you doing?"

"I will not lose to a *snail*!" Guy replied through gritted teeth.

Hands tightly gripping the wheel, Guy pushed forward, sailing past Turbo. He chuckled as he pulled ahead of the snail.

But he wasn't out of danger yet. Guy's back tire

shredded through a thick patch of marbles and then locked up. He lost control, swerving wildly into Turbo's path and smashing into the lapped cars.

Wham! Wham! Wham! Horrified, Turbo watched as cars collided all around him. Within seconds a pile of smoke and steel burned on the track, blocking the path of the oncoming cars. Turbo revved his engine, looking for a way through—

And then everything went black.

Never Give Up!

Turbo slowly opened his eyes. Through a blur he could see mounds of twisted, smoking metal all around him. Racers shouted and argued, trying to escape their trapped cars. Slick oil leaks painted the asphalt.

"What the . . . where am I?" Turbo asked in a shaky voice.

He blinked, and his vision cleared a little. In front of him he could see the finish line less than a yard away.

Relieved, Tito spotted Turbo at the edge of the collision. Chet saw him too.

"Let's finish this," Turbo said, starting to rev up.

But nothing happened.

Confused, Turbo tried to rev up again, but there was no blue light, no humming motor sound. He stretched an eyestalk behind him and saw that his shell had been badly damaged. It wasn't just cracked—a large piece of his shell was missing.

Turbo's heart sank as reality hit him. He had lost his powers!

His friends all looked on, shocked.

"Oh no," Whiplash said.

"Turbo," Tito said sadly.

Turbo turned back and looked at the finish line. It might have only been three feet away, but for a regular snail it was like a football field. He'd never make it. With a heartbroken sigh, he retreated into his shell.

The Indy 500 fans watched Turbo on the giant TV screen. Chet had never seen his brother give up before. Even before he got his superspeed powers, he'd never let anything stop him. He couldn't stop now.

"No, no, no! What are you doing? Don't give up!" Chet pleaded.

He rushed toward his brother, but smacked into

the glass trapping him. How frustrating! Chet had to do something.

He nervously peered down at what lay beyond the glass. He was only a few inches from the edge of the table. If he pushed hard enough . . .

Chet didn't have time for fear. He pushed the glass with all his might, inching closer and closer to the table's edge. Then . . .

Crash! The glass fell to the floor with a clatter, but Chet was all right. He scooted out and headed for the window of the VIP box. He'd made it all the way to the window when he heard a voice behind him.

"Hey, where are you going?" Danny asked.

Chet looked down over the window ledge at the speedway. Everything he had spent his whole life avoiding was down there: people, cars, crows, and salty food. But he had to help his brother. Taking a deep breath, he bolted down the other side of the window.

"Come back here! Wait!" Danny yelled.

He reached over the window, grabbing for Chet. Thinking quickly, Chet used his mouth to grab the string of a balloon passing by, and it carried him over the crowd.

"Nooo!" Danny wailed.

As Chet soared over the spectators, he twisted his body to direct the balloon toward the racetrack.

"Theoooo!" Chet called out.

The other snails saw him. "Whoa, is that Chet?" Burn asked.

Now the balloon was bouncing Chet on the heads of the racing fans. He dodged a salty pretzel, but in the next instant, someone opened a can of soda, spraying him and sending him and the balloon spiraling away. Then . . .

Squawk! Chet looked up and saw three crows overhead, diving right for him!

"Are you *kidding* me?" Chet asked.

Chet screamed. But as the crows got closer, he saw that they had been taken over by Whiplash, White Shadow, and Burn. The snails had tied up their beaks using lanyards as reins.

"Long time, no see, Chet!" Whiplash said with a grin.

With that, White Shadow's crow zipped past and popped Chet's balloon. Chet tumbled down, landing on a series of power lines crisscrossing the track. He tucked into his shell and rolled down the lines, tumbling out right at Tito's feet. Then he climbed onto the wall of the pit.

"Theo! Theo!" he called.

His voice echoed inside Turbo's shell. Turbo slowly emerged, looking left and right until he saw Chet on the wall of the pit.

"Turbo," Chet said.

Turbo stared at his brother. It was the first time Chet had called him by his racing name.

"Finish this," Chet said.

Turbo looked back at his damaged shell, and then to Chet. "I can't."

"Yes, you can. It's in you," Chet insisted. "It's *always* been in you. I did not just face every fear known to snailkind to watch you hide away in your shell. My little brother never gives up. That's the best thing about you. So you get out there and you finish this . . . *Turbo*."

Turbo's heart swelled with newfound confidence. Chet believed in him. Chet, his brother, his best friend, believed in him.

Eyes narrowed with determination, Turbo began to make his way along the track with his own power. The cameras picked it up, plastering him on every video screen in the speedway.

"Wait a minute. I don't believe it . . . ," the announcer said. "It appears Turbo has decided this race is *not* over."

A chant began to spread throughout the stadium.

Turbo . . . Turbo . . . Turbo . . .

Turbo inched his way forward when something spurred him to look over his shoulder. Guy was on his feet, straining to push his car out of the tangled heap of metal. He locked eyes with Turbo. Then, with a last massive push, he flipped his car back on its wheels. He quickly hopped inside and pumped the gas pedal.

Boom! A cloud of smoke erupted from the exhaust as the engine gave out.

Relieved, Turbo kept going, inching closer and closer to the finish line. But Guy was not about to give up. He climbed out of his car, and with one hand on the steering wheel he forcefully pushed his car forward.

"Unbelievable! The race is back on!" the announcer crowed.

Sweat poured from Guy's forehead as he struggled forward. Slime dripped from Turbo as he slowly pushed ahead.

"Hey snail! He's gaining on you!" Kim-Ly warned.

A tire broke free from Guy's car. Turbo saw it just in time and dodged it, but Guy was closer now.

With all his might, Turbo kept going. He managed to keep a few inches between him and Guy's race car. Victory was so close. . . .

Guy saw it too. Blinded with rage, he began to stomp furiously, trying to crush Turbo.

"*Turbo!*" Chet yelled. "*Tuck and roll!*"

Turbo did it. He pulled his body inside his shell, and the extra weight rolled the shell forward . . . and right over the finish line!

"And Turbo wins it by a shell!" the announcer cheered.

Tito leaped over the pit wall, holding Chet as Turbo emerged from his shell, beaming.

"Turbo!" Chet called out. Tito fought his way through the crowd and lowered Chet next to Turbo.

"We won, right? We just won?" Chet asked.

"We won," Turbo replied.

"Woo-hoo!" Chet cheered. He wrapped his eyestalks around Turbo and hoisted him off the ground. "Hey, everybody! My brother won the Indy 500!"

Tito turned to the nearest camera. "Hey, Angelo, we did it!"

Tito lifted Turbo high in the air. "It's like I always said, little amigo. You are *amazing*!"

Moments later they were all standing in Victory Lane. Turbo perched on the trophy, and Tito raised it high in the air. Turbo swelled with happiness. His dream had come true! Even if he never raced again, he'd always have this moment.

Hometown Hero Returns!

Two weeks later the snails were back in California, perched on top of a shiny new shooting star sign at Starlight Plaza. But things looked a lot different than the first time Turbo had seen the plaza.

A long line of people waited at the taco shop. Inside, Angelo cooked up tacos on a shiny new oven. Bobby's hobby shop was full of kids and their pet snails, getting shells from Bobby and having them decorated by Kim-Ly. Paz's garage was full of customers.

"Man, look at this place!" Burn exclaimed.

"This joint is jumpin'!" Smoove Move observed.

Whiplash turned to Turbo. "I gotta admit . . . ya did good, garden snail."

Turbo smiled. "Well, I had a pretty good crew. Little abusive, but pretty good."

A blast of music entered the parking lot, and the snails looked down to see Tito's totally tricked-out new taco truck pull in. Racing flames streaked across the side, floodlights jutted out from the hood, and hubcap spinners sparkled in the sunlight.

The auto shop, the nail salon, and the hobby shop were all filled with customers.

Tito parked, and Paz opened the back of the truck to reveal a spectacular snail racetrack. Gone were the old battered toy tracks; the new track had loops, flags, lights, and even a ring of fire.

"All racers to the starting line!" Paz called out.

The snails looked at Turbo with concern. He still wore a bandage over his broken shell.

"You okay getting down there without your super-powers and stuff?" Burn asked.

"Don't worry, I'll be careful," Turbo said. Then, without warning, he jumped!

Whomp! A tiny parachute ejected from his shell, and he gently floated to the ground. The other snails followed, using parachutes made from candy wrappers and other paper scraps.

Tito plucked Turbo from the air. "You didn't think I'd let you race looking like that, did you?" he asked. He opened up his other hand, revealing a snazzy new racing shell. He peeled off Turbo's bandage. "You won't miss this."

Then his expression changed. "What?"

Turbo bent his eyestalk to look at his shell. The hole had healed up!

"You're all better!" Tito cried.

He placed Turbo back down on the starting line just as the sound of a siren blared. Everyone turned to see Chet scoot up. He had a new shell that looked like an ambulance, and he made siren noises with his mouth.

"Okay, listen up. Let's have a nice, safe race out there today. Don't want any accidents!" he announced. Then he winked at Turbo. "That being said, blow 'em off the track, bro."

Burn sidled up to Chet. "Mmm, I love a man in uniform, for real!"

Chet blushed, but he was smiling. "I'm on duty here."

Burn joined the other snails on the starting line. Whiplash glanced at Turbo.

"Nice shell," he said. "But can it do this?"

He nodded to Burn. Her shell rumbled, and real flames shot out of her exhaust pipes!

Then four monster truck wheels popped out of White Shadow's shell. Whiplash revealed a functioning turbine engine. High-powered speakers rotated out of Smoove Move's shell, blasting music. And Skidmark's rear wing transformed into the spinning blade of a high-powered fan.

Turbo watched, wide-eyed, as they all started revving their high-powered engines. Bobby, Kim-Ly, and Paz had given them all a supercharged makeover.

"On your mark . . . get set . . . blast off!" Paz yelled.

Turbo watched his friends take off . . . and then he felt something stir inside him. He looked at his shell and saw a familiar blue glow shining brighter and brighter. A sly grin spread across his face as he revved his engine.

Zoom! Turbo rocketed down the track . . . and into a future fueled for speed.

PERFORM AWESOME STUNTS WITH THE TURBO TEAM IN THE NEW VIDEO GAME!

DREAMWORKS

TURBO
SUPER STUNT SQUAD

RACING INTO STORES JULY 2013